Made in United States
Orlando, FL
08 April 2024

45599293R00068